Millions of Americans remember Dick and Jane (and Sally and Spot too!). The little stories with their simple vocabulary words and warmly rendered illustrations were a hallmark of American education in the 1950s and 1960s.

But the first Dick and Jane stories actually appeared much earlier—in the Scott Foresman Elson Basic Reader Pre-Primer, copyright 1930. These books featured short, upbeat, and highly readable stories for children. The pages were filled with colorful characters and large, easy-to-read Century Schoolbook typeface. There were fun adventures around every corner of Dick and Jane's world.

Generations of American children learned to read with Dick and Jane, and many still cherish the memory of reading the simple stories on their own. Today, Pearson Scott Foresman remains committed to helping all children learn to read—and love to read. As part of Pearson Education, the world's largest educational publisher, Pearson Scott Foresman is honored to reissue these classic Dick and Jane stories, with Grosset & Dunlap, a division of Penguin Young Readers Group. Reading has always been at the heart of everything we do, and we sincerely hope that reading is an important part of your life too.

THE ULTIMATE Dick and Jane

STORYBOOK COLLECTION

Published in the United States by Grosset & Dunlap,
an imprint of Penguin Random House LLC
345 Hudson Street, New York, New York 10014

Designed by Irene Vandervoort

Printed and manufactured in China

ISBN 978-0-448-44856-5 9 10

CONTENTS

We Look and See

We Look and See

by WILLIAM S. GRAY, DOROTHY BARUCH,
and ELIZABETH RIDER MONTGOMERY

Illustrated by Eleanor Campbell

BASIC READERS: CURRICULUM FOUNDATION PROGRAM
The 1946-47 Edition

Scott, Foresman and Company

CHICAGO ATLANTA DALLAS NEW YORK

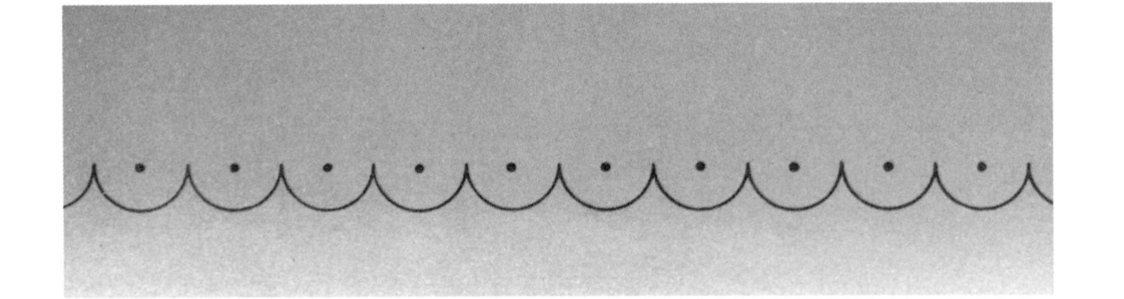

Stories

Dick

Look, look.

Oh, oh, oh.

Look, look.
Oh, look.

Jane

See, see.
See Jane.

Oh, Jane.
Look, look, look.

Oh, oh, oh.

Oh, see.

Oh, see Jane.

Funny, funny Jane.

Baby

Look, Dick.

Look, Jane.

Look and see.

See Baby.

See, see.

Oh, oh, oh.

Oh, Dick.

Look and see.

See Baby.

Look, Jane, look.

See Baby.

Oh, oh, oh.

Funny, funny Baby.

Spot

Come, Dick.

Come and see.

Come, come.

Come and see.

Come and see Spot.

Look, Spot.
Oh, look.
Look and see.
Oh, see.

Run, Spot.

Run, run, run.

Oh, oh, oh.

Funny, funny Spot.

Puff

Jump, Puff.
Jump, jump, jump.

Run, Puff.

Run and jump.

Run, run, run.

Jump, jump, jump.

Oh, oh, oh.

Oh, Puff.

Look and see.

Oh, oh, oh.

Oh, see.

Tim

Jump up, Baby.
Jump up.
Up, up, up.
Jump up.

Come up, Tim.

Come up.

Up, up, up.

Come up.

Look, Dick, look.
See Baby and Tim.
Funny Baby.
Funny Tim.

Tim and Spot

Go up, Tim.

Go up.

Go up, up, up.

Go down, Tim.

Go down.

Go down, down, down.

Oh, Jane.

See Spot and Tim.

See Spot run.

Funny, funny Spot.

Funny, funny Tim.

Up and Down

Come, Puff.

Come and go up.

Go up, up, up.

Come down, down, down.

Go up and down.

Up and down.
Up and down.
Go up, up, up.
Come down, down, down.

Oh, Baby.

See Puff jump.

See Puff run.

Oh, oh, oh.

See Puff jump and run.

Puff and Dick

Come, Baby.
Run, run.
Run and see.

Look up, Baby.
Look up and see Puff.

Look up, Baby.

Look up and see Dick.

See Dick go up.

See Dick go up, up, up.

Oh, Jane.

See Dick come down.

See Puff come down.

Down, down, down.

Oh, oh, oh.

See Puff come down.

Look and See

Look, Spot.

Look, Puff.

Look and see.

See Baby and Tim.

Come, Spot, come.

Jump up.

See Puff jump.

Jump up, Spot.

Jump up and see.

Come, Dick, come.

Come and see.

See Spot and Puff.

See Baby and Tim.

Look, look.

Look and see.

See Baby Go

Look, Spot, look.
See Tim and Puff.
Jump, Spot, jump.
Jump up.
Jump up.

Oh, Jane.

Look and see.

See Baby go.

See Tim go.

See Spot and Puff go.

Oh, Dick.

Look, look.

Look and see.

See Spot jump.

See Puff jump.

Oh, oh, oh.

We Come and Go

We Come and Go

by WILLIAM S. GRAY, DOROTHY BARUCH,

and ELIZABETH RIDER MONTGOMERY

Illustrated by Miriam Story Hurford

BASIC READERS : CURRICULUM FOUNDATION SERIES

Scott, Foresman and Company

CHICAGO ATLANTA DALLAS NEW YORK

Stories

Go, Go, Go

See, see.
See Mother go.

Go, Baby Sally.
Go, Sally, go.

See Dick go.
See Jane go.
Go, go, go.

Oh, Dick.

See Baby Sally.

See Baby Sally go.

Oh, oh, oh.

Go, Dick, go.

Oh, Mother.

See Dick and Jane.

Oh, oh, oh.

Tim and Baby Sally

Oh, Tim.

Mother sees something.

Dick sees something.

Jane sees something.

Look, look.

Baby sees something.

Tim sees something.

Oh, oh.

Baby wants something.

Tim wants something.

Oh, look, look.

Look, Mother.

Look, Dick and Jane.

See Tim.

Oh, oh, oh.

Puff and Spot

Baby Sally said, "Look, look.
Look and see.
See Spot and Puff.
Spot wants something.
Puff wants something."

Jane said, "Look, Mother.
Spot wants something.
Puff wants something."

Dick said, "Oh, oh.
Funny, funny Spot.
Funny, funny Puff."

Sally said, "Look, Mother.
Look, Dick and Jane.
Look and see.
Oh, see."

Come and Jump

Dick said, "Come, Father.
Come and jump."

Jane said, "Jump, Father.
Jump, Father, jump."

Sally said, "Come, Mother.
Come and see Father.
See Father jump and play.
Oh, oh.
Father is funny."

Jane said, "Oh, Father.
Mother can jump.
Mother can play."

"Oh, oh," said Baby Sally.
"Mother can jump and play.
Oh, oh.
Mother is funny."

Dick said, "Come, Puff.
Come, Spot.
Come and play."

Sally said, "Run, Puff.
Run, Spot.
Run, run, run.
Run and jump."

Dick said, "See Puff.
Puff can play.
Puff can run and jump."

Jane said, "Oh, oh.
Spot can not play.
Spot can not run.
Spot can not jump.
Spot is funny."

Come and See

Father said, "Come, Dick.
Come, Jane.
Come and see something."

Sally said, "Run, run.
Run and see it.
It is down, down, down."

Father said, "Look, Baby.
Up it comes.
Up, up, up.
See it work."

Baby Sally said, "Oh, oh.
See it work.
Work, work, work."

Dick said, "See it work.
See it go down, down.
Down, down.
See it go down."

Jane said, "Look, Baby.
See Tim go down.
Oh, oh, oh."

Sally said, "I see Tim.
Tim is down, down, down.
Jump down, Father.
Jump down, Dick.
I want Tim."

Father said, "Oh, Baby.
Dick can not jump down.
I can not jump down."

Jane said, "Oh, oh.
I see Tim.
I see Tim come up."

Father said, "Oh, look.
Up comes Tim."

Spot and the Ball

Dick said, "Come, Jane.
Come and play.
Come and play ball."

Jane said, "Oh, Dick.
I can not find the ball.
Come, Dick, come.
Come and find the ball."

Dick said, "I see it.
I see the big ball."

Jane said, "Oh, Dick.
I want the little ball.
Find the little ball."

Dick said, "Look, Jane.
I can find the big ball.
Spot can find the little ball."

"Oh, oh," said Jane.
"See Spot run.
Spot wants the little ball.
Spot is funny."

Come and Help

Jane said, "Run, Dick.
Run to Mother.
Run and help Mother work."

Mother said, "Come, come.
Come to me.
Come and help me.
Come and help me work."

Baby Sally said, "Oh, Mother.
Sally is big.
Sally wants to work.
Sally wants to help."

Mother said, "Run, Sally.
Run to the car.
Run to the car and help me.
Big, big Sally can help me."

"Oh, oh," said Baby Sally.
"I see something in the car.
It is little Puff.
Puff wants to go.
Puff wants to go in the car.

Oh, oh.
Little Puff can go.
Little Puff can go in the car."

We Go Away

Dick said, "Spot wants to go.
Spot wants to go in the car."

Father said, "Down, Spot.
Run away, Spot.
You can not go.
You can not go in the car."

Jane said, "We can go.
Mother is here.
Father is here.
Dick is here.
Sally is here.
Away we go."

Dick said, "Spot is not here.
Puff is not here."

Jane said, "Puff is here.
Puff is here in the car."

Sally said, "Come, Puff.
Jump up to me.
You can go.
You can go in the car."

Dick said, "I see something.
Look down, Jane.
Look down and see something.
It is funny.
Can you see it?"

"Oh," said Jane.
"Here is Spot."

Jane said, "Come in, Spot.
Come in.
You can go.
You can go in the car."

"Away we go," said Sally.
"Away we go in the car.
Mother and Father.
Dick and Jane.
Spot and Puff.
Tim and Baby Sally."

Something for Spot

"Cookies," said Sally.
"I see three big cookies."

"Three big cookies," said Jane.
"Three big cookies for me."

"Cookies, cookies," said Dick.
"Three big cookies for me."

Sally said, "Three big cookies.
See the three big cookies.
One for Dick and one for Jane.
One for me and one for Spot."

Dick said, "Oh, Baby.
Where is the cookie for Spot?
Where, oh, where?
Where is the one for Spot?"

Sally said, "Here, Spot.
Here is a cookie for you."

"Oh, oh," said Jane.
"Where is a cookie for Baby?"

Mother said, "Here is one.
Here is a cookie for Baby.
A big, big cookie for Baby."

Sally Sees the Cars

Jane said, "Look, look.
I see a big yellow car.
See the yellow car go."

Sally said, "I see it.
I see the big yellow car.
The yellow car can go away.
The yellow car can go, go, go."

Dick said, "I see a blue car.
See the blue car go.
See the blue car go away."

Sally said, "Oh, Dick.
I want to go in the blue car.
I want to go away.
Away, away, away."

"I see a boat," said Sally.
"I see a big red boat.
I want to go in the red boat.
I want to go away in it."

Dick said, "See the boat go.
See the red boat go away.
You can not go away in it.
You can not go away."

Jane said, "Look up, Baby.
You can see something.
It is red and yellow.
It can go up, up, up.
It can go away."

Sally said, "I want to go.
I want to go in it.
I want to go up.
Up, up, away."

Dick said, "Come to me, Baby.
Here is something red and blue.
You can go up in it.
Jump in, jump in."

Sally said, "See me go up.
See me go down.
Up and down.
Up and down.
See me go."

Three Big Cookies

Jane said, "Come and play.
We can make something.
I can make cookies.
I can make three big cookies."

Sally said, "I can make cookies.
I want to make little cookies.
One, two little cookies."

"See my cookie," said Dick.
"Here is a funny cookie.
One big funny cookie."

Sally said, "See, see.
We can make cookies.
One funny cookie.
One, two little cookies.
One, two, three big cookies."

"Oh, look," said Sally.
"See Spot jump."

"Oh, oh," said Dick.
"Where is my funny cookie?
Where, oh, where?
Where is it?"

We Make Something

Dick said, "I can make a house.
A big house for two boats.
See my house.
The blue boat is in it.
The yellow boat is in it."

Jane said, "I can make a house.
A little house for three cars.
See my house."

Sally said, "I can make a house.

A big house for Tim.

Here is my house.

Tim is in it.

Tim can play in it.

Oh, oh.

Tim looks funny."

Jane said, "See Puff and Spot.
Puff and Spot want to play."

Dick said, "Look, look.
Down comes my big house."

Jane said, "Oh, look.
Down comes my little house."

Sally said, "Oh, oh, oh.
Down comes my house for Tim.
Down, down, down."

Spot Finds Something

Dick said, "Come here.
Come and help me.
I can not find the two boats.
I can not find my red ball.
Where is my little red ball?
Where is my yellow boat?
Where is the blue boat?
Where, oh, where?"

Jane said, "I can help you.
I can find two boats for you.
Here is one yellow boat.
Here is one blue boat."

Sally said, "I see three cars.
Here is my red car.
Here is my blue car.
Here is my yellow car.
One, two, three cars."

Dick said, "Oh, my.
See Spot work.
Spot can help me.
Spot can find something."

Sally said, "Look, look.
Spot can find Tim.
Oh, oh.
Spot is funny."

The Blue Boat

Dick said, "Oh, Father.
We want to go in a boat.
Here is a blue boat.
We want to go in it."

Sally said, "Go, go.
We want to go.
We want to go in a boat.
In the big blue boat."

Father said, "You can go.
You can go in the boat.
Jump in, jump in.
Jump in the big blue boat."

Sally said, "Here we go.
Here we go in the boat.
In the big blue boat."

Jane said, "I see two big boats.
A big red boat.
And a big yellow boat."

Sally said, "One, two.
I see two big boats.
A big red boat.
And a big yellow boat."

Dick said, "I see two little boats.
Two little blue boats."

"Oh, my," said Sally.
"Tim is not here.
Where is Tim?
Oh, Father.
Help me.
Help me find Tim."

Jane said, "Look, Sally.
See Spot jump in.
Spot can find Tim for you."

Dick said, "Oh, oh.
See Spot go."

Jane said, "See Spot.
Here comes Spot to the boat."

"Oh, Spot," said Baby Sally.
"You can find Tim.
You can help me."

THE NEW BASIC READERS
THE NEW We Work and Play

THE NEW

We Work and Play

The 1956 Edition

William S. Gray, Marion Monroe,

A. Sterl Artley, May Hill Arbuthnot

Illustrated by Eleanor Campbell

SCOTT, FORESMAN AND COMPANY

Chicago, Atlanta, Dallas, Palo Alto, New York

Stories

Work

Work, Dick.
Work, work.

See, see.

See Dick work.

Oh, Dick.

See, see.

Oh, oh, oh.

See Sally Work

Work, work, work.
Sally can work.
See Sally work.

Oh, Dick.

Oh, Jane.

See, see.

Sally can work.

Oh, Sally.

Funny, funny Sally.

Oh, oh, oh.

Play

Oh, Father.
See funny Dick.
Dick can play.

Oh, Mother.

Oh, Father.

Jane can play.

Sally can play.

Oh, Father.

See Spot.

Funny, funny Spot.

Spot can play.

Look

Look, Jane.

Look, look.

Look and see.

See Father play.

See Dick play.

Look, Mother.

Look, Mother, look.

See Father.

See Father and Dick.

Oh, Mother.

See Spot.

Look, Mother, look.

Spot can help Dick.

Run and Help

Run, Jane.
Help Mother.
Run, Jane, run.
Help Mother work.

Come, Sally, come.

Come and help.

Come and help Mother.

Run, run, run.

Look, Sally, look.

See Spot work.

Funny, funny Spot.

Oh, oh, oh.

Spot can help Mother.

Puff

Look, Dick.

See Puff jump.

Oh, look.

Look and see.

See Puff jump and play.

Come, Jane, come.

Come and see Puff.

See Puff jump and run.

See funny little Puff.

Oh, oh, oh.

See little Puff run.

Oh, see Puff.

Funny little Puff.

Spot and Tim and Puff

Spot can jump.
Little Puff can jump.
Look, Tim, look.
See Spot and Puff play.

Look, Tim.

See Sally jump.

See Sally jump down.

Down, down, down.

Sally can jump and play.

Oh, Puff.

See funny little Tim.

See Tim jump down.

Down, down, down.

Tim can jump and play.

Big and Little

Come, come.

Come and see.

See Father and Mother.

Father is big.

Mother is little.

Look, Father.

Dick is big.

Sally is little.

Big, big Dick.

Little Baby Sally.

Oh, look, Jane.

Look, Dick, look.

Sally is big.

Tim is little.

Big, big Sally.

Little Baby Tim.

The Funny Baby

Come down, Dick.

Come and see.

See the big, big mother.

See the funny little baby.

Puff is my baby.

Puff is my funny little baby.

I see the big mother.
I see the little baby.
Look, Jane.
See the big father.

Look, Dick, look.

See something funny.

See my baby jump.

See my baby jump down.

See my baby run.

Oh, oh, oh.

Something Blue

Oh, Jane, I see something.

I see something blue.

Come, Jane, come.

Come and see Mother work.

Mother can make something.

Something blue.

Look, Mother, look.

I can work.

I can make something.

I can make something yellow.

Look, look.

See something yellow.

Oh, Jane, I can work.
I can make something blue.
I can make something yellow.

Oh, see my funny Tim.
Little Tim is yellow.
Baby Sally is blue.

The Little Car

Oh, oh, oh.

See my red car.

See my yellow car.

Come, Father, come.

Help Baby Sally.

Oh, Father.

I see my blue car.

I see my yellow car.

Look, Father, look.

Find my little red car.

Help Sally find the red car.

Look, Father.

I see the red car.

I can find the little red car.

See my cars.

Red and blue and yellow.

Red and blue and yellow cars.

Spot Helps Sally

Look, Spot, look.
Find Dick and Jane.
Go, Spot, go.
Help Sally find Dick.
Help Sally find Jane.

Go, Spot.
Go and find Dick.
Go and find Jane.
Run, Spot, run.
Run and find Dick.
Run and find Jane.

Oh, oh, oh.

Spot can find Dick.

Spot can find Jane.

Oh, oh.

Spot can help Sally.

Spot can play.

The Big Red Boat

Come, Baby Sally.

Come and see Father work.

See Father make boats.

Look, Sally.

The little boat is my boat.

I can make my boat blue.

See my little blue boat.

Look, Sally, look.
See my big boat.
I can make my boat red.
Look, Sally.
See my boat.
See my big red boat.

Oh, look, look.

See Puff jump.

See my boat go down.

Oh, look.

My boat is yellow.

The Boats Go

Oh, Dick.

The blue boat can go.

The yellow boat can go.

My little red car can go.

Look, look.

See my red car go.

Oh, oh.
See my red car.
See my red car go down.
Down, down, down.

Oh, Dick.
Help, help.
My little red car is down.

Up, up, up.

Up comes the little red car.

Look, Baby Sally.

See Dick help.

See the little red car come up.

Up, up, up.

The little red car is up.

Something Funny

Oh, Dick, look.

I can make Tim and Puff.

Tim is yellow.

Puff is red.

Make something, Dick.

Make something yellow.

Make something blue.

I can make something blue.
I can make blue cars.
I can make blue boats.

See my cars and boats.
See the funny blue boat.
See the funny blue car.

Look, Jane, look.

Up go the boats.

Up go the cars.

Up, up, go Tim and Puff.

Down come the boats.

Down come the cars.

Down comes Tim.

Down comes Puff.

Down,

down,

down.

THE NEW BASIC READERS

Guess Who

Dick

Look, Dick.
Look, look.

Oh, oh.
Look, Dick.

Oh, oh.
See Dick.
Oh, see Dick.

Sally

Look, Sally.
Look, look.
See Jane.

Oh, Jane.

See Sally.

See little Sally.

Little, little Sally.

Look, Jane.

See funny Sally.

Oh, oh, oh.

Funny little Sally.

Help, Help

Look, Dick.

See Spot.

Oh, see Spot.

Help, help.

Oh, Jane.

See Spot.

Oh, see Spot.

Come, Jane, come.

Help, help, help.

Look, Dick.

See Spot and Sally.

Come see Sally.

See funny little Sally.

Sally Sees Something

Come, Sally.
Come and look.
Come and see Sally.
Funny little Sally.

Dick, Dick.

Help, help.

I see something.

Help, help, help.

I see something.

Look, Sally.

I see something.

I see Baby Sally.

Little Baby Sally.

Look, look.

See funny Baby Sally.

Something Funny

Look, Dick.

Look, look.

I see something funny.

Come and see.

Come and see Spot.

Oh, Jane.

I see something funny.

Come, Jane, come.

See Spot and Baby Sally.

Come and help.

Look, Dick.

See Jane help Spot.

Oh, see something funny.

See little Spot.

Funny little Spot.

Jane and Puff

Oh, Jane.

I see something.

Look, Jane, look.

Look here.

Come, Puff.

Come here.

Jump, little Puff.

Jump, jump.

Look, Baby Sally.
Come here and look.
See Puff.
Puff can help.
Puff can help Jane.

See Puff Go

Come here, Dick.

Come and see Puff.

See Puff play.

See Puff jump.

Puff can jump and play.

Oh, Mother, Mother.
Come and look.
See Puff jump and play.
See little Puff play.
Look, Mother, look.
See Puff jump and play.

Oh, oh, oh.

See Puff jump down.

See Puff jump and go.

Jump down, funny Puff.

Jump down.

Jump down.

Go, go, go.

Tim and Sally Help

Sally said, "Look, Mother.
I can help.
See Baby Sally help.
See little Tim help.
See little Tim go.
Oh, see little Tim go."

Sally said, "Look, Tim.
Look down here.
I see cookies.
I see cookies down here.
Cookies, cookies, cookies."

Sally said, "Come, Mother.
We can go.
Look here, Mother.
Cookies, cookies, cookies.
Come, Mother, come.
We can go."

Go Away, Spot

Dick said, "Down, Spot.
I can not play.
Down, Spot, down.
Go away, little Spot.
Go away and play."

Sally said, "Oh, Spot.
We see you.
Tim and I see you.
And little Puff sees you.
We see you, funny Spot."

Dick said, "Oh, oh, oh.
Go away, Spot.
You can not help.
You can not play here."

Sally said, "Run away, Spot.
Run, run, run."

Puff, Tim, and Spot

Sally said, “See Puff go.
Puff can jump down.
Puff can run away.
See little Tim.
Tim can not jump down.
Tim can not run away.”

Dick said, “Come, Spot.
You and I can play.
Look here, Spot.
Cookies, cookies.
Jump, Spot, jump.”

Dick said, “See Spot.
Oh, see Spot jump.”

Jane said, “Mother, Mother.
We see something funny.
Come here.
Come here.
Come and see Spot.”

Find Dick

Jane said, "I see you.

I see you, Sally.

I can find you.

I can not find Dick.

Help me, Sally.

Come here.

Help me find Dick."

Jane said, "Oh, Father.
I can not find Dick.
And we can not play.
Help me, Father.
Help me find Dick."

Father said, "Look, Jane.
Look, look, look.
You can find Dick."

Sally said, "Oh, oh.
I see Dick now.
Father and I see Dick.
We see funny Dick.
Look, Jane, look.
You can find Dick now."

Who Can Help?

Dick said, “Mother, Mother.
Come here.
I want you.
Come and help me.
Oh, Jane.
Oh, Father.
Who can come?
Who can come and help me?”

Dick said, "Go away, Spot.
You can not help me.
Oh, my.
Oh, my.
I want Mother.
Mother can help me.
Run, Spot, run.
Run and find Mother."

Dick said, "Oh, Spot.
Now I can come in.
You can help me.
Little Spot can help.
You can help me come in."

See What I See

Dick said, "Look, Sally.
Look down here.
See what I see.
See my big cookie.
See me and my big cookie.
You can see Spot here.
Spot wants my big cookie."

"Oh, oh," said Sally.
"I see Tim and me.
And now I see Puff.
Puff is in here.
I see little Puff.
Puff and Tim and me."

Sally said, "Look, Jane.
Look down here.
You can see Jane in here."

Jane said, "Oh, oh, oh.
Who sees what I see?
It is something funny.
It is not Jane."

Little Boat

Sally said, "See my boat.
I want my little boat.
I want my little boat in here."

Jane said, "Dick can get it.
Dick is big.
Dick can go and get it."

"Not now," said Dick.
"I can not get it now."

Jane said, “Come, Sally.
Come and play.
Here is Tim.”

“I want my boat,” said Sally.
“Who can get it for me?
Is Father here?
Father can get it for me.”

Sally said, "Oh, oh, oh.
Come here, Dick.
See what I see.
See my little blue boat now.
See who wants my boat.
My little blue boat.
See who wants it now."

What Can Dick Make?

Jane said, "Look, Sally.
See what I can make.
It is big and yellow.
It is for Puff."

Sally said, "Look, Mother.
I can make something for Tim.
Jane can make something for Puff.
What can Dick make?"

Dick said, “I can make something.
Come and see what it is.”

“Is it blue?” said Sally.
“Is it yellow?
Is it red?”

Dick said, “Oh, my.
It is red and yellow and blue.
Come and see what it is.”

Jane said, "Look, Sally.
Dick can make something pretty.
See what Dick can make."

"I see it," said Sally.
"It is pretty.
What is it?"

Jane said, "Oh, Sally.
It is Dick."

See It Go

Father said, “Look in here.
You can find something.
Something you want.”

Dick said, “Look, Jane, look.
Red, yellow, and blue.
Yellow is for me.
Who wants red and blue?”

Jane said, “I want blue.
Red is for Sally.”

Dick said, “Come, Sally.
Come and get something.
Red for you and blue for Jane.”

Sally said, "Oh, Dick.
Pretty, pretty.
Make it big.
Make it big, big, big."

Jane said, "Run, Spot.
Run away, Puff.
See what I see.
Run, run, run."

“Now look,” said Dick.
“See my boat.
See my boat go.
I can make it go away.
See it go.
Oh, see it go.”

Who Can Work?

Dick said, "See me work.
I can help Father.
I can get something.
Something for Father."

Dick said, "Look, Father.
Jane plays and plays.
You and Mother work.
And I work.
Jane can not work.
Jane is a little baby."

Father said, "Oh, Dick.
Jane is not a baby."

Jane said, "See me now.
I can do something.
See me work.
I can help Mother.
See what I can do.
Sally is a baby.
Sally can not work."

Mother said, "Oh, my.
Sally is not here.
Who can find Sally?"

Sally said, "Look, Mother.
See me in my little house.
I can work.
And Spot and Puff can work.
We can make a house.
A funny little house."

Find My Ball

Sally said, “I want my ball.
My pretty yellow ball.
Who can find it for me?”

Jane said, “Here is a ball.
See this blue ball, Sally.
Do you want this ball?”

Sally said, “I want my ball.
My ball is yellow.
It is a big, pretty ball.
And it is in this house.
Help me find it.”

“It is not here,” said Dick.

Sally said, "Where is my ball?
It is in this house.
Where, oh, where is it?"

"It is not here," said Dick.
"Not down here, Sally."

Sally said, "Oh, Spot.
Do you see my ball?
Where is it, Spot?
Go and get it."

Sally said, "Oh, Jane.
Look up.
Look up.
See where my ball is.
Oh, oh, oh.
Dick looks down.
Little Spot looks up.
And Spot finds my ball.
My pretty yellow ball."

A Big Red Car

Dick said, “Away I go.
Away in my big red car.
See me go, Sally.”

Sally said, "I want a car.
Make two cars, Dick.
A car for you.
And a car for me.
Make two cars."

Dick said, "Oh, Sally.
You can come in my car.
In my big red car."

"I want a car," said Sally.
"Make one for me, Dick.
A little one for me."

Dick said, "Look, Sally.
I can do something.
See what I can do.
I can make a big, big car.
Two can get in this car now."

Dick said, “Here, Sally.
This will look pretty in my car.
I will make it go up for you.
See it go up, up, up.
Now get in my car.”

“Away we go,” said Sally.
“Away, away in a big red car.”

Who Will Jump?

Dick said, “Look, Sally.

Do you see this?

Come with me.

You will see something funny.”

Sally said, "Oh, Dick.
I see what you want to do.
You want to make me jump.
Oh, oh.
You want to make me jump."

Dick said, "Not you, Sally.
I want to find Jane.
I want to make Jane jump."

Sally said, “I see Jane.
Jane is in the house.
Oh, oh.
I want to go in the house.
I want to see Jane jump.”

“Come with me,” said Dick.
“Come in the house with me.
You will see something fun.
You will see Jane jump.”

Dick said, "Now look, Sally.
Now you will see Jane jump.
One . . . Two . . ."
"Three," said Sally.
"One, two, three.
See Dick jump."

I See You

Jane said, "Come with me, Sally.
Come to the house with me.
Dick will not look here.
Not in the house.
Dick will not find you here."

Dick said, “Oh, oh.
I see something blue.
I can guess where Jane is.
One, two, three for Jane.
I see you, Jane.
One, two, three for you.
Come with me, Puff.
We want to find Sally now.
Where, oh, where is Sally?”

Dick said, "Oh, oh.
I see something yellow.
I can guess where Sally is.
One, two, three for Sally.
I see Sally with Jane.
One, two, three for Sally.
Now, little Puff.
Do you want to come with me?
We will get Jane and Sally."

Jane said, "One, two, three.
One, two, three for me.
And one, two, three for Sally.
Sally is with me."

Dick said, "Oh, funny me.
This is something yellow.
It is not Sally.
And this is something blue.
It is not Jane."

Guess Who

Sally said, "See the cars.
See the cars go up, up, up.
One, two, three.
Three little yellow cars."

Father said, "Oh, Baby Sally.
You can not play here.
This is where we work.
Here is a ball.
Run and play with the ball."

Mother said, "Spot, Spot.
Go to the house.
You can not play here.
Come with me to the house."

Jane said, "Come here, Dick.
Oh, come here.
Guess what I see.
Guess what Spot can make."

Sally said, "Oh, pretty, pretty.
Spot can make something pretty.
I can do what Spot can do.
I can make something pretty."

Jane said, "Oh, Father.
I want to do it."

Father said, "Come, Dick.
You and Jane can do it.
And here is little Puff.
I will help Puff do it."

Dick said, “Look, Mother.
See what we can make.
Guess who this is.”

“Guess who this is,” said Jane.

“Guess who this is,” said Sally.
“And see the two little ones.
Guess who.
Guess who.”

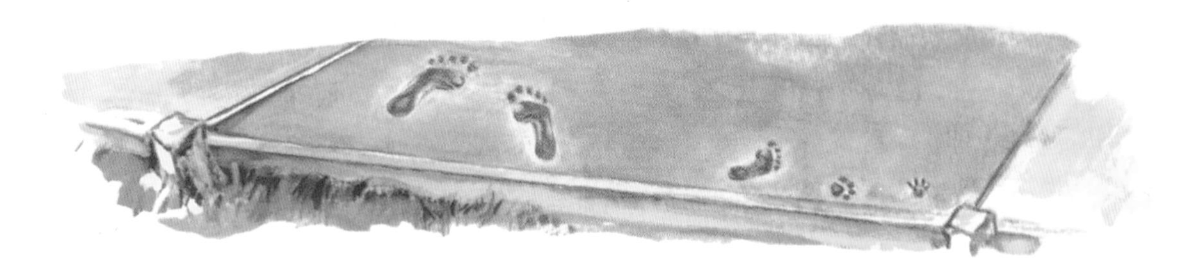

THE NEW BASIC READERS
THE NEW We Come
and Go

Come

Come, Sally.
Come, come.

Oh, Sally.

Come, come.

Come, Sally, come.

Oh, see.
See Sally go.

Go, Sally, go.
Go, go, go.

See Jane Go

Oh, Sally.
See Jane go down.
Down, down, down.
See Jane go down.

Look, Jane.
Look, look.
Oh, look.

Look, Tim, look.

Oh, look.

See funny, funny Jane.

See funny Jane go.

Sally and Mother

Sally said, "Oh, see.
See Mother go.
Come, Dick.
Come, Jane.
Come and go."

Jane said, “Oh, Dick.
See Sally and Tim.
Oh, oh, oh.
See Baby Sally go.
Go, Dick, go.”

Sally said, "Oh, Mother.
See Dick go down.
See Jane go down.
Funny, funny Dick and Jane."

Tim and Baby Sally

Sally said, "Oh, Tim.
I see something.
Mother sees something.
Dick and Jane see something."

"Oh, oh," said Sally.
"I see something.
Something for Baby Sally.
And something for little Tim."

Sally said, “I see something.
Something for Dick and Jane.
And something for Sally.
I want something for Tim.”

“Oh, look,” said Dick.
“See something for little Tim.”

Spot and Puff

Baby Sally said, "Look here.
I see something funny.
I see Spot and little Puff.
Spot wants something.
Puff wants something."

Jane said, "Look, Mother.
See Spot and Puff.
Spot and Puff want something."

Mother said, "Run, Jane.
Run, Dick.
Run and help little Sally.
Sally wants help."

"Oh, oh," said Baby Sally.
"Oh.
Oh.
Oh."

Little Tim Can Help

Dick said, "Look, look.
Here we come.
We can help."

Jane said, "Run, Dick.
Run, run.
We can help."

"Look, here," said Sally.
"One is for Dick.
One is for Jane.
And one is for Baby Sally."

"Look, Mother," said Sally.

"Here we come.

See little Tim.

Tim can help.

Tim can help Mother.

Oh, oh.

Tim is funny."

I See Three

"Here, Dick," said Mother.
"Here is something."

"I see three," said Dick.
"We want three.
I want a big one.
Jane wants a big one.
Sally wants a little one."

“One, two, three,” said Jane.
“A big one for Dick.
A big one for Jane.
A little one for Baby Sally.
One, two, three.”

“Oh, oh,” said Sally.
“One, two, three.
One, two, three.”

"See, see," said Father.
"One, two, three.
I see something funny."

"Run, run," said Sally.
"Here we come."

Father said, "Oh, oh.
Here I go."

Jump and Play

Sally said, "Oh, look.
Mother can jump.
Mother can jump and play."

Dick said, "Jump, Father.
You can jump.
You can jump and play."

"Look, Mother," said Sally.
"See Father jump.
See Father jump and play.
Big, big Father is funny."

Jane said, "Oh, Father.
You can not jump and play.
Spot can not jump and play."

Dick said, "Oh, see Puff.
Puff can jump.
Puff can jump and play."

We Make Something

"Look here," said Dick.
"I can make something funny.
I can make Spot.
Spot is red and blue."

"Oh, Dick," said Jane.
"I want to make something.
I want to make something blue."

"Look, Sally," said Jane.
"See my funny blue Puff.
Make something, Sally.
Make something blue."

"Oh, Jane," said Sally.
"I can not make Puff.
I can not make Spot.
I want to make little Tim."

"See me work," said Sally.
"I can make something blue.
See my funny blue Tim."

"Look, Sally," said Jane.
"Here is something for Tim.
Here is a funny red mother.
And a funny blue father.
A father and mother for Tim."

Play Ball

"Come, Jane," said Father.
"Come and play ball.
Come and play."

"Oh," said Jane.
"See the red ball go.
See it go up, up, up.
Run, Dick, run."

"Oh, oh," said Dick.
"Where is my ball?
I can not find it.
Come here, Jane.
Run and help me.
Help me find my red ball."

"I can help you," said Jane.
"We can find the red ball."

Dick said, "I see it.
I see the red ball.
Look, Father.
See where it is.
Come and help me."

Jane said, "Oh, Dick.
Spot can help you.
Spot can find the red ball."

Spot Finds Something

Dick said, "Come and work.
Come and help me.
I can not find the two boats.
I can not find my red ball.
Where is my yellow boat?
Where is the blue boat?
Where is my little red ball?
Where, oh, where?"

Jane said, "I can work.
I can find two boats.
Here is the yellow boat.
Here is the blue boat."

Sally said, "I can find cars.
See my little yellow car.
See my red car and my blue car.
Where is the red ball?
Where is my little Tim?"

Dick said, "Spot can work.
Spot can find the red ball.
Spot can help me."

Sally said, "See Spot work.
Spot can find Tim.
Spot can help me."

Down It Comes

Dick said, “I can make a house.
A big house for two boats.
A house for the yellow boat.
And for the blue boat.
See my big house.”

Jane said, “I can make a house.
A big house for three cars.
Red and blue and yellow cars.”

Sally said, “I can make a house.

A little house for Tim.

Here is my house for Tim.

Tim is in it.

Tim can play in it.

Oh, oh, oh.

Tim looks funny in the house.”

"See my house," said Dick.
"Down it comes."

"Oh, see my house," said Jane.
"Down, down it comes."

"Oh, oh, oh," said Sally.
"Down comes my little house.
Run away, Puff.
Run away, Spot.
You can not play here."

Away We Go

Sally said, "Away we go.
Away we go in the car.
Mother and Father.
Dick and Jane.
Sally and Tim."

Dick said, "Spot is not here.
Puff is not here."

Dick said, "I see something.
Look down, Jane.
Look down and see something.
It is funny.
Can you see it?"

"Oh, oh," said Jane.
"Here is Spot."

"Come in, Spot," said Jane.
"You can go in the car."

"Away we go," said Sally.
"Away we go in the car.
Mother and Father.
Dick and Jane.
Sally and Tim and Spot.
Away we go in the big car."

Three Big Cookies

“Cookies, cookies,” said Sally.
“One, two, three cookies.
Three cookies for me.”

“Three big cookies,” said Jane.
“Three big cookies for me.”

“Cookies, cookies,” said Dick.
“Three big cookies for me.”

"Cookies, cookies," said Sally.
"See the three big cookies.
One for Dick and one for Jane.
One for me and one for Spot."

Dick said, "Oh, you funny baby.
Where is the one for Spot?
Where, oh, where?"

“Here, Spot,” said Sally.
“Here is a cookie for you.”

“Oh, oh,” said Jane.
“Where is one for Sally?”

“Here it is,” said Mother.
“Here is a cookie for Sally.
A big, big cookie for Sally.”

See It Go

Jane said, "Look, look.
I see a big yellow car.
See the yellow car go."

Sally said, "I see it.
I see the big yellow car.
I want to go away in it.
I want to go away, away."

Dick said, “Look up, Sally.
You can see something.
It is red and yellow.
It can go up, up, up.
It can go away.”

Sally said, “I want to go up.
I want to go up in it.
I want to go up, up, up.
I want to go away, away.”

"Look, Sally," said Dick.
"Here is Father in a boat.
You can go away in it."

"Jump in, jump in," said Father.
"Jump in the big blue boat."

"We can go," said Sally.
"We can go away in a boat.
Away in a big blue boat."

The Blue Boat

Jane said, “See the red boat.
See the yellow boat.”

Dick said, “I see the two blue boats.
Two little blue boats.”

Sally said, “I see the boats.
A big yellow boat.
A little red boat.
And two blue boats.
Yellow, red, and blue.”

"Oh, my," said Baby Sally.

"Tim is not here.

Where is Tim?

Oh, Jane.

Help me.

Help me find Tim."

"Look, Baby Sally," said Jane.
"See Spot jump in.
Spot can find Tim for you."

"Oh, oh," said Dick.
"See Spot go."

"Here comes Spot," said Jane.
"Here comes Spot to the boat."

"Oh, oh," said Baby Sally.
"Here comes Spot.
And here comes Tim."

THE NEW BASIC READERS

THE NEW We Look and See

Look

Look, look.

Oh, oh, oh.

Oh, oh.
Oh, look.

Jane

Oh, Jane.

Look, Jane, look.

Look, look.
Oh, look.
See Jane.

See, see.

See Jane.

Oh, see Jane.

Dick

Look, Jane.

Look, look.

See Dick.

See, see.

Oh, see.

See Dick.

Oh, see Dick.

Oh, oh, oh.

Funny, funny Dick.

Sally

Look, Dick.
Look, Jane.
See Sally.

Oh, oh, oh.

Oh, Dick.

See Sally.

Look, Jane.
Look, Dick.
See funny Sally.
Funny, funny Sally.

Oh, See

Look, Sally, look.
Look down.
Look down, Sally.
Look down, down, down.

Look up, Sally.

Look up, up, up.

Run, Sally, run.

Run and jump.

Run and jump up.

Look, Jane.
Look and see.
Oh, see.
See funny, funny Sally.